D0500778

# Chicken Break!

## A Counting Book

Cate Berry illustrated by Charlotte Alder

Feiwel and Friends
New York

**One** chicken, standing guard.

**Two** chickens scan the yard.

**Three** chickens hatch the plan.

**Four** chickens on the lamb.

**Five** chickens tippy TIPtoe.

**Six** chickens incognito.

**Seven** chickens smuggle the code.

**Eight** chickens press "upload."

**Nine** chickens man the gate.

**Ten** chickens peck . . . and wait . . .

TOP SECRET!

"Chickens make a
CHICKEN BREAK!"

TOP SECRET
PRETZ
TOP SECRET!
MAP
TOP SECRET!

OF THE
OPERA
ADMIT ONE
OF THE
OPERA
ADMIT ONE

**Ten** chickens droop and drag.

**Nine** chickens hail a cab.

**Eight** and **seven** squish inside . . .

Up on top, **six** now ride.

**Five** chickens launch jet packs.

**Four** chickens zip-line back.

**Three** tunnel underground . . .

**Two** chickens skydive down.

**One** chicken leads the flock,

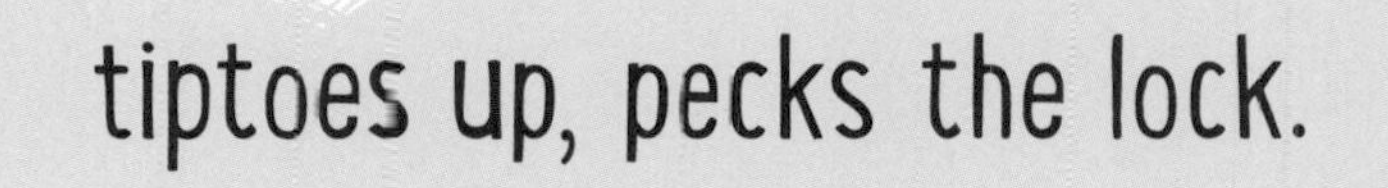
tiptoes up, pecks the lock.

Chickens waddle to the coop,
C

shushing, clucking, one last poop.

Huddle tighter, big tail shake,